IMAGINE THAT

Licensed exclusively to Imagine That Publishing Ltd
Tide Mill Way, Woodbridge, Suffolk, IP12 1AP, UK
www.imaginethat.com
Copyright © 2019 Imagine That Group Ltd
All rights reserved
4 6 8 9 7 5 3
Manufactured in China

Illustrated by Gareth Llewhellin
Adapted from 'The Velveteen Rabbit' by Margery Williams

ISBN 978-1-78700-895-3

A catalogue record for this book is available from the British Library

The Velveteen Rabbit

by Margery Williams

Adapted from 'The Velveteen Rabbit' by Margery Williams
Illustrated by Gareth Llewhellin

There was once a Velveteen Rabbit,
and in the beginning he was really splendid.
He was fat and bunchy, as a rabbit should be;
his coat was spotted brown and white,
he had real thread whiskers,
and his ears were lined with pink satin.

For at least two hours the Boy loved him, and then his friends arrived for his birthday party and in the excitement of looking at all of the new presents, the Velveteen Rabbit was forgotten.

For a long time, the Velveteen Rabbit lived
in the nursery toy cupboard, and no one
thought very much about him.

He was naturally shy and, being only
made of velveteen, some of the more
expensive toys snubbed him.
The mechanical toys thought they
were very superior.
They looked down on the other toys and
pretended they were real.

The Velveteen Rabbit could not claim
to be real, for he didn't know that
real rabbits existed.

'What is REAL?' asked the Velveteen Rabbit one day,
when he was lying beside Rocking
Horse on the nursery room floor.
'Does it mean having things that buzz
inside you and a stick-out handle?'

'Real isn't how you are made,'
said Rocking Horse.
'It's a thing that happens to you.
When a child loves you for a long,
long time, not just to play with,
but REALLY loves you,
then you become real.'

There was a person called Mum who ruled the nursery.
Sometimes she took no notice of the playthings lying about,
and sometimes, for no reason whatsoever, she went swooping
about like a great wind and hustled them away into cupboards.
She called this 'tidying up', and the playthings all hated it,
especially the metal ones.

The Velveteen Rabbit didn't mind it so much,
for wherever he was thrown he always landed softly.

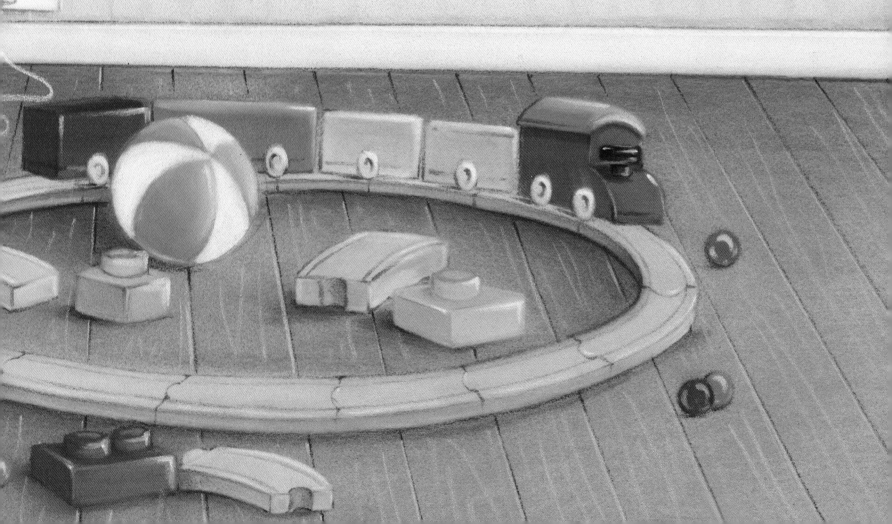

One evening, when the Boy was going to bed, he couldn't find the cuddly teddy that always slept with him. His mum was in a hurry and, seeing that the toy cupboard door stood open, she reached inside.

'Here,' she said, 'take your old bunny!
He'd like to sleep with you!'
And she dragged the Velveteen Rabbit out by
one ear and placed him into the Boy's arms.

That night, and for many nights after,
the Velveteen Rabbit slept in the Boy's bed.
At first he found it rather uncomfortable,

for the Boy hugged him very tight, he rolled over on him,

and sometimes he pushed him so far under the pillow that the Velveteen Rabbit could scarcely breathe.

But very soon the
Velveteen Rabbit
grew to like it,
for the Boy used
to talk to him,

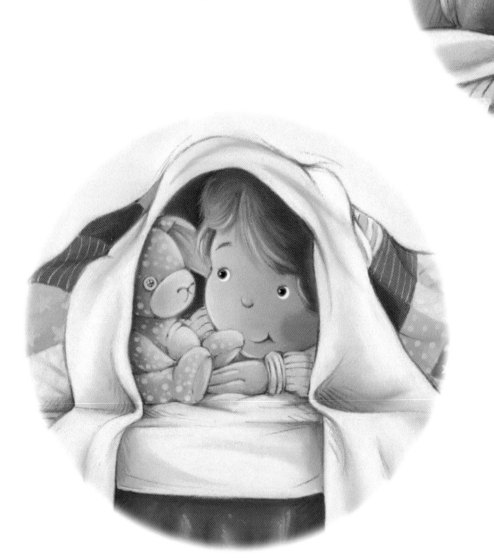

and made nice tunnels
for him under the
bedclothes that he said
were like the burrows
that real rabbits lived in.
And they had splendid
games together.

And when the Boy dropped off to sleep, the Velveteen Rabbit would snuggle down close under his little warm chin and dream, with the Boy's hands cuddling him all night long.

Soon spring came and they spent long days together in the garden.

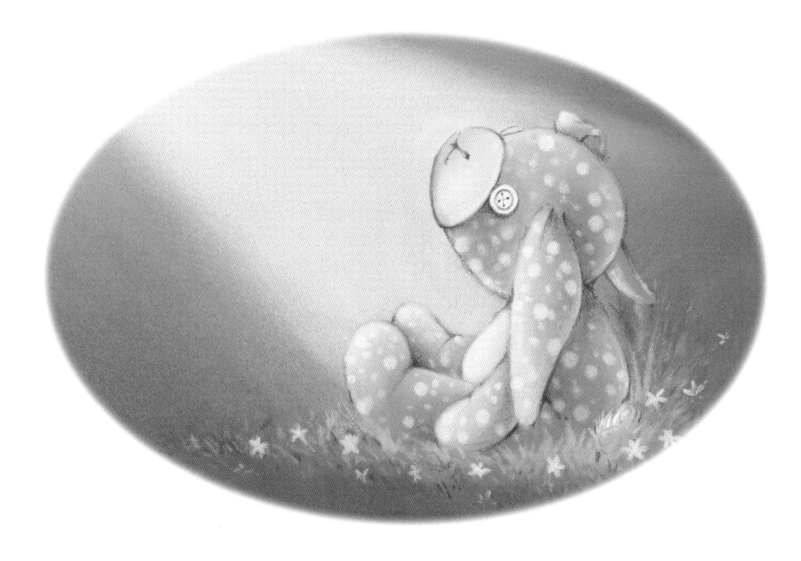

Once, when the Boy was called away suddenly to
go in for dinner, the Velveteen Rabbit was left out
on the lawn until long after dusk.
The Boy couldn't go to sleep without the Velveteen Rabbit and
Mum had to come and look for him with a torch.

'You must have your old bunny!' she said.
'Fancy all that fuss for a toy!'

The Boy sat up in bed and stretched out his hands.

'You mustn't say that', said the Boy.
'He isn't a toy. He's REAL!'

When the Velveteen Rabbit heard what the Boy said
he was happy, for he knew what Rocking Horse
had said was true at last.
The nursery magic had happened to him,
and he was a toy no longer …

… he was real.